Nate The Great
and The
Halloween
Hunt

Nate the Great
and The
Halloween Hunt

by Marjorie Weinman Sharmat
illustrations by Marc Simont

A Yearling Book

Published by
Yearling
an imprint of
Random House Children's Books
a division of Random House, Inc.
New York

Visit us on the Web! www.randomhouse.com/kids

Educators and librarians, for a variety of teaching tools, visit us at www.randomhouse.com/teachers

ISBN: 0-440-40341-3
Reprinted by arrangement with the Putnam Publishing Group, Inc., on behalf of Coward-McCann, Inc.
Printed in the United States of America
One Previous Edition
September 2005
40 39
UPR

For Fritz,

who loved to greet

all the ghosts and goblins

$\mathbf{M}$y name is Nate the Great.

I am a detective.

Tonight I got into trouble.

Tonight I was locked in a haunted house

with my dog, Sludge.

I was in big trouble.

There were no pancakes there.

I was on a case.

A Halloween case.

It started about an hour ago.

My dog, Sludge, and I were
looking out our window.

We were waiting for witches and clowns
and Draculas and princesses
to ring our doorbell.

Suddenly I heard a scratch at the door.

A loud scratch.

I went to the door
and opened it.

Someone was standing there
in a long dress, a bonnet, and shawl.

It was Little Red Riding Hood's

grandmother,
carrying a Trick or Treat bag
in her big teeth.
His big teeth.
The grandmother was Annie's dog,
Fang.

I, Nate the Great, did not think
that Halloween was a scary holiday.
Until now.
"Where is Annie?" I asked him.
"Does she know you're out alone
on Halloween?"
I did not wait for an answer.
I dropped some treats into Fang's bag.

He wagged his tail and

went down the walk.

I closed the door behind him.

Sludge crawled out from under a chair.

I said to him,

"Be brave on Halloween.

We do not believe in

ghosts and goblins.

Or grandmothers with big teeth."

Sludge went back to the window.

The doorbell rang.

I opened the door.

Annie and Rosamond were outside.

They were both dressed as

Little Red Riding Hood.

And they were each carrying a basket

covered with a red cloth.

"Your grandmother was just here,"
I said to both of them.

"I know it," Annie said.

"This is Fang's first year
out alone on Halloween."

"I put some treats in his bag," I said.

"And now I'll give you some
for your baskets."

"My basket is already heavy
with treats," Rosamond said.

"I can't carry any more."

"Mine isn't full yet," Annie said.

She lifted the napkin from her basket,

and I dropped some treats inside.

"I am finished with Trick or Treating,"
Rosamond said.
"I came here to ask
for your help."
"What kind of help?"
"One of my cats, Little Hex,
is missing," Rosamond said.
"He hates Halloween.
Every year he tries to hide.
But this year I can't find him."
"Where are your other three cats?"
I asked.
"Perhaps Little Hex is with them."
"Oh no," Rosamond said.
"Every Halloween
Super Hex, Big Hex, and Plain Hex

go to the old haunted house
on the next street and help to haunt it.
But Little Hex is too scared,
so he hides."
"Wait until tomorrow," I said.
"Halloween will be over,
and Little Hex will come out
of his hiding place."
"But he might be really lost,"
Rosamond said.
"I'm so worried

I can't eat any of my treats.
Please help me."
"Very well. I, Nate the Great,
will take your case.
Tell me, when was the last time
you saw Little Hex?"
"He was following Annie and me,"
Rosamond said.
"Where did you go tonight?" I asked.
"First I put on my costume,"
Rosamond said, "and then I went to

Annie's house.

Little Hex followed me there."

"And then what?"

"Annie finished dressing up Fang.

She sent him on his way.

Then Annie and I went to

Claude's house. He gave us some

cookies.

We put them in our baskets.

Next we went to Esmeralda's house.

She gave us her special

Halloween biscuits."

"Was Little Hex still following you?"

"Yes," Rosamond said.

"Then Esmeralda asked Annie and me

to help her get into her gorilla costume.

So Annie and I stepped into her house.

And Little Hex did too.
Annie and I helped
Esmeralda become a gorilla.

The three of us started
to leave Esmeralda's house.
That's when I noticed
that Little Hex was gone."
"Then he's probably still
in Esmeralda's house," I said.
"No, we looked everywhere
in her house," Annie said.
"Was Esmeralda's door open or closed
while you were helping her
with her costume?" I asked.
"Open," Annie said.
"So Little Hex probably

escaped outside," I said.

"It is hard to find
a small black cat in the dark.
But I will go out and hunt for him."

"Oh, thank you," Rosamond said.

"I will go home and wait
for you to bring him back."

Rosamond and Annie left.

I wrote a note to my mother.

Dear mother,
I am on a Halloween case.
I am hunting for little Hex
who would rather hide than hunt.
I will be back (unless a
grandmother with big teeth
uses them on me)
Love,
Nate the Great

I got a flashlight.

Sludge and I went out into the night.

I saw two pirates ahead of us.

"Excuse me," I said, "have you

seen Rosamond's cat, Little Hex?"

The pirates turned around.

They were Finley and Pip.

"We have just started
on our rounds," Finley said.
"And all we've seen
are a dancing artichoke and a robot."

Sludge and I walked
up and down the street.
We saw more pirates.
And monsters and kings
and artichokes.
But we did not see Little Hex.
Where could he be?
"What would a scared cat do
on Halloween?" I asked Sludge.
Then I had an idea.
*Perhaps Little Hex wasn't scared
anymore.*
Perhaps I should be looking
for a brave cat
and not a scared one.
"Perhaps this year

Little Hex is learning how to haunt,"
I said to Sludge.
"I, Nate the Great,
don't believe in haunted houses.
But we must go to that old house
and hunt for Little Hex."
Sludge did not look happy.
But we walked to the old house.

It looked haunted.

It looked like every ghost

who had ever haunted anything

was haunting this house

on this night.

Sludge and I crept up the front steps.

They creaked.

I knew they would.

I knocked on the door.

It creaked.

I knew it would.

I opened the door.

It squeaked.

I knew it would.

I stepped into the house.

Sludge slunk in.

I called out,

"Super Hex, Big Hex, Plain Hex,

Little Hex, any Hex, are you here?

You have one minute to show your

faces. Then Sludge and I are leaving."

I started to count the seconds.

"One, two, three, four . . ."

SLAM!

The door shut behind us.

I tried to open it.

It was stuck.

"There must be another door,"

I said to Sludge.

I flashed my flashlight around.

I saw cobwebs, and old furniture

draped with white sheets.

I heard clinking and clanking
and shrieking.
"Is that you, cats?" I shouted.
I saw three pairs of eyes
glowing at me in the dark.
Cats' eyes.
They belonged to Super Hex, Big Hex
and Plain Hex.
Then they disappeared.
I flashed my flashlight
all over the house.

The three cats were gone.

But how did they get out of the house?

How could Sludge and I get out?

I heard more clinks and clanks

and shrieks.

The cats had left,

so what was making

those ghostly noises?

I, Nate the Great,

now believed in haunted houses.

We had to get out of here!

I found another door.

It was locked.

I tried windows.

They were locked.

"There must be a way out," I thought.

"The cats got in and got out."
I kept looking.
And then, in front of me
I saw a ghost!
I don't believe in ghosts,
so how could I see one?
But it was creeping toward me
dressed in a white sheet.
And suddenly I knew
I had solved the case.
Little Hex must be under that sheet,
learning how to haunt.

I lifted the sheet.

Sludge was huddled under it.

He was hiding.

I unwrapped him.

He led me to another room.

He found a hole.

It was small.

But he dug in it, making it bigger.

It was big enough for us to crawl into.

It led to the outside.

We were free.

"Good work, Sludge," I said.

We walked down the street,

away from the house.

We were happy to do that.

"Little Hex was not

in the haunted house," I said.

"We are back to looking

for a scared cat."

Did I have any clues?

Pancakes help me think.

Bones help Sludge think.

We went home.

We ate.

I thought back.

The last time Rosamond saw Little Hex

was when he followed her into
Esmeralda's house.

Then he was gone.

Esmeralda and Annie and Rosamond
had searched Esmeralda's house.

But they could not find Little Hex.

So he must have gone out
into the night.
Alone.
But why would he do that
when he was scared of Halloween?
Sludge was scared of Halloween, too.
He had hidden under a chair
in my house and under a sheet
in the haunted house.
Perhaps Little Hex was hiding
under something.
But where?
"We must go where Little Hex
was last seen," I said.
Sludge and I went
to Esmeralda's house.

She was there,

eating from her bag of treats.

"I am looking for Little Hex," I said.

"He isn't here," Esmeralda said.

"Rosamond and Annie and I looked all

over this house.

Want some of my treats?

My bag got too heavy to carry

around."

I stared at Esmeralda's treats.

Suddenly I remembered something.

I remembered lots of things.

I remembered *clues*.

"I have no time for treats," I said.

"I must go to Rosamond's house

right away."

Sludge and I rushed
to Rosamond's house.
She was lying on a sofa.
She was still wearing her
Little Red Riding Hood costume.
She looked strange in it.
Rosamond looked strange in everything.
"I was just at Esmeralda's house,"
I said. "She was eating
some of her treats."
"I'm still not hungry," Rosamond said,
pointing to her covered basket
on a table. "I'm too sad to eat."
"I think I know where Little Hex is,"
I said.
"Where? Where is he?"

Rosamond clutched her red cloak.
I, Nate the Great,
walked over to Rosamond's basket.
I lifted up the red cloth that
was on top of it.

And there was Little Hex,
fast asleep in the basket!
"It's Little Hex!" Rosamond cried.
"Yes," I said. "I, Nate the Great,
say that you've been carrying him

around ever since you left
Esmeralda's house."

"I *have?*"

"Yes. He must have crawled
into your basket at Esmeralda's house
while you and Annie were busy
helping Esmeralda become a gorilla."

"But how could he fit inside?"
Rosamond asked.

"Where are the treats I collected?"

"There are a few left in the basket,"
I said. "Little Hex probably ate
most of them
and took their place
under the napkin
and hid there.

Sludge hid under a chair
and a sheet tonight.
When you're scared,
you might hide under something.
Sludge gave me that clue twice."
Rosamond stroked Little Hex.
"But how did you know that
Little Hex was hiding
in my basket?" she asked.
"He could have been hiding anywhere."
"You gave me the clue," I said.

"You told me that you and Annie
started out together,
doing Trick or Treat.
When you got to my house,
Annie had room in her basket
for treats, but you said
your basket was too heavy.
How come your basket
was heavier than Annie's?
They should have been the same
because you both went to
the same places.
I, Nate the Great,
say that your basket
was full of Little Hex
and he was full of your treats.

No wonder it was heavy."

"I'm so happy to have

Little Hex back," Rosamond said.

"Let's have a Halloween party

to celebrate.

I'll go outside and invite

everybody I see."

"Including your grandmother

with the big teeth?" I asked.

"Sure," Rosamond said.

"Fang probably collected more treats

than anybody."

"I believe that," I said.

"But I will never be

hungry enough to take

food from Fang's fangs."

Sludge and I left.

The case was over.

Halloween was almost over.

No more hunting, no more haunting.

What had caused all the

clinking and clanking

and shrieking

in that old haunted house?

I would never know.

I, Nate the Great, say that some mysteries are better left unsolved.

~~ Extra ~~
Fun Activities!

What's Inside

Nate knew about Halloween. He knew about cats. He knew there was more to know. He read some books. This is what he learned.

NATE'S NOTES: Halloween Facts

The first Halloween was in Ireland. The holiday started almost 3,000 years ago! Some things have changed. For example, people used to carve TURNIPS—not pumpkins.

Halloween is sweet. Each year during Halloween, Americans buy one-quarter of all the candy sold all year.
Happy trick-or-treating!

Dracula is a good costume. Of course, vampires are just pretend. And bats don't drink blood, right?
Actually—WRONG.

Three species of bats DO drink blood. (The other 197 species DON'T.) The three species of "vampire" or blood-drinking bats are the common vampire bat, the white-winged vampire bat, and the hairy-legged vampire bat. Good news: None of the blood drinkers live in the United States. They live in Central and South America. Also, they rarely attack humans.

The world's biggest pumpkin weighed 1,446 pounds!*

* More giant pumpkin info on pages 26–28.

Trick-or-treating began in the United States just 75 years ago. The Boy Scouts helped start it.

Where's my candy? Nine out of ten parents sneak goodies from their kids' trick-or-treat bags!

Some kids collect money for UNICEF on Halloween. UNICEF is a charity. It helps kids around the world. Want to join in? Go online and register. UNICEF will send you a collection box. The Web site is www.unicefusa.org/trickortreat.

In Mexico, October 31 starts a holiday called the Day of the Dead. In Spanish, it's el Día de los Muertos. This holiday honors dead people! Mexican kids create altars with photos and candles. They decorate graves with flowers. They sing songs. They munch on candy skulls. It's not a scary holiday. It's fun!

The magician Harry Houdini died on Halloween in 1926. Houdini was an escape artist. He got out of a locked crate thrown into a river. He broke out of jail cells. He even escaped from a coffin. Pretty spooky! Magicians are still trying to discover Houdini's secrets.

NATE'S NOTES: Stuff About Cats

Here's another clue that Rosamond is weird. Hex is NOT a normal cat name. Popular names for girl cats are Sassy, Misty, and Princess. For boy cats: Max, Sam, and Charlie.

Ancient Egyptians had the first pet cats. That was more than 4,000 years ago. The Egyptians even turned cats into mummies! They believed cats were a kind of god.

At some times in history, people thought of cats as witches' best friends. Witches liked black cats best. That's why people say black cats are bad luck. At least, SOME people say that. Here are some other ideas:

The Scottish believe that if you see a strange black cat walking on your porch, you will become rich.

Italians say it's good luck when a cat sneezes.

Some Dutch people avoid talking about private stuff with a cat in the room. They believe cats spread gossip.

Cats have 230 bones. That's 24 more than humans. Cats' hearts beat about twice as fast as humans'.

The nose pad of a cat is unique, just like the fingerprint of a human.

When a cat is frightened, the hair all over its body stands up. When a cat is ready to attack, just the hair on its back stands up.

Some people keep cats to kill mice. One cat named Towser killed 28,899 mice in 21 years. That's about four mice per day every day.

House cats can sprint at about 30 miles per hour. They can jump five times their height. They are good at surviving falls. But they do NOT always land on their feet. They can break bones if they fall more than about 24 feet.

Cats would not make good detectives. They are too lazy. They sleep about 16 hours a day. They spend one-third of their waking hours grooming.

The world's longest cat lives in Chicago. His name is Leo. He is 48 inches long. That's about as tall as an eight-year-old kid. Me-ow!

Top 20 Halloween Costumes

Check out the most popular Halloween costumes.
Notice: Fang did not make the list.

1. Spider-Man
2. Princess
3. Witch
4. Vampire
5. Monster
6. SpongeBob SquarePants
7. Ninja
8. Athlete
9. Ghost
10. Power Ranger

11. Angel
12. Pumpkin
13. Batman
14. Yugi, Tea, or another character from *Yu-Gi-Oh!*
15. Singer
16. Barbie
17. character from the Harry Potter books
18. Pirate
19. Clown
20. Firefighter

How to Make Your Own Face Paint

Fun for Halloween. Good for disguises.

GET TOGETHER:

- 3 tablespoons diaper cream or Eucerin
- 6 small paper cups
- red, yellow, and blue gel food coloring*
- craft sticks

* Get permission first. Some food coloring may tint your skin a bit. Do a test to make sure your paint won't stain your skin too much.

MAKE YOUR FACE PAINT:

1. Divide the diaper cream or Eucerin among three cups.
2. Add a few drops of red food coloring to one cup. Stir with a craft stick. If the color is too pink, add another drop of coloring. Stir again. Repeat until you like the color.
3. Use the same technique to make cups of blue and green paint.
4. Experiment! Mix the red, blue, and yellow together to make other colors in the remaining cups.
5. Paint some faces! See the next page for one idea. Or create your own design.

red + yellow = orange
yellow + blue = green
blue + red = purple

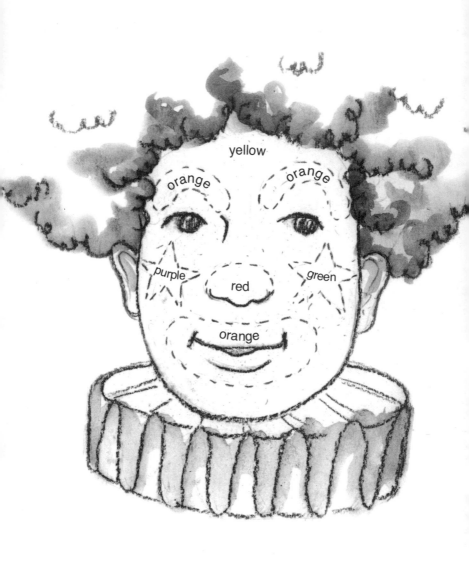

How to Make Frozen Hand Fruit Punch

Serve this punch at a Halloween party. Your friends will give you a hand.

Serves 20.

STEP ONE: Make the Frozen Hands

GET TOGETHER:

- 3 or 4 rubber gloves
- dish soap and a sponge
- water
- rubber bands
- 4 clothespins

MAKE YOUR HANDS:

1. Wash the gloves thoroughly with soap. Carefully rinse off all the bubbles.
2. Fill the hand part of a glove with water.
3. Wrap a rubber band around the open part of the glove.
4. Place the glove in the freezer. If possible, use a clothespin to clip it to a freezer shelf. Hang it with the fingers pointing down.
5. Repeat for the other gloves.
6. Leave the gloves in the freezer for at least one day. (You can do STEP TWO while you wait.)

STEP TWO: Make the Punch

GET TOGETHER:

- a large bowl
- a big spoon
- 1 package strawberry Kool-Aid
- 1 package cherry Kool-Aid
- 2 cups sugar
- 3 quarts water
- 1 6-ounce can frozen orange juice
- 1 6-ounce can frozen lemonade
- 1 liter ginger ale

MAKE YOUR PUNCH:

1. In the bowl, mix together everything but the ginger ale.
2. Just before serving, add the hands. Get the gloves out of the freezer. Quickly run them under warm water. Peel off each glove. (It's okay if some of the fingers break off. Hands missing fingers look extra creepy!)
3. Pour in the ginger ale.
4. Serve. Drink. Make ghoulish jokes. Blah-ha-ha!

Halloween Jokes

Q: What do ghosts serve on Halloween?
A: Ice scream.

Q: What is a witch's favorite subject?
A: Spelling.

Q: Why are mummies good students?
A: They get wrapped up in their work.

Q: What kind of music do mummies like?
A: Wrap!

Q: What is a vampire's favorite holiday?
A: Fangsgiving!

How to Make Shrunken Heads

Scarier than a jack-o'-lantern!

Ask an adult to help you.

GET TOGETHER:

- one apple for each head
- an apple peeler
- a knife
- 4 cups water
- 2 tablespoons salt
- a small bowl
- a plate
- craft eyes, cotton balls, and glue (if you want to decorate your head)

MAKE YOUR SHRUNKEN HEAD:

1. Peel the apple.
2. Have an adult help you use the knife to carve eyes, a nose, and a mouth into your apple. Watch your fingers!
3. Put the water and salt in the bowl. Stir well.
4. Place the apple in the salt water for 24 hours.

5. Take the apple out of the water. Put it on the plate. Find it a safe place away from pets. Let it dry for up to two weeks.
6. If you want, decorate your head. Place craft eyes in the "eye sockets." Glue cotton on top to make "hair."
7. Spook your friends!

Weird Facts About Giant Pumpkins

From 1979 to 1982, a farmer named Howard Dill grew the world's biggest pumpkins. He spent 30 years breeding them to make them bigger. Now Dill sells pumpkin seeds on the Internet. They cost up to $8 each.

In 1996, two people grew huge pumpkins. They weighed more than 1,000 pounds each. Each year, pumpkins get bigger! In 2004, the world record was 1,446 pounds. That pumpkin weighed about as much as a cow.

Growing giant pumpkins is a fun hobby. It's also serious business. One contest pays $50,000 for the biggest pumpkin.

Growers work hard. They dig huge growing pits. They mix batches of fertilizer and manure. They build shelters. Some put in cameras to protect their pumpkins from animals and vandals. And they water their pumpkins a *lot*—up to 1,000 gallons per day!

A giant pumpkin can grow 20 pounds a day. The stress can cause them to split—or even explode! That's bad news for the grower. Winning pumpkins cannot have any splits.

What can you do with a giant pumpkin?
- Display it at a Las Vegas casino!
- Get it on TV!

One thing you *can't* do: make a giant pie. Giant pumpkins don't taste good. And they're not good *for* you. That's because growers use lots of chemicals to kill pumpkin-eating bugs.

Have you helped solve all
Nate the Great's mysteries?

❑ **Nate the Great**: Meet Nate, the great detective, and join him as he uses incredible sleuthing skills to solve his first big case.

❑ **Nate the Great Goes Undercover**: Who— or what—is raiding Oliver's trash every night? Nate bravely hides out in his friend's garbage can to catch the smelly crook.

❑ **Nate the Great and the Lost List**: Nate loves pancakes, but who ever heard of cats eating them? Is a strange recipe at the heart of this mystery?

❑ **Nate the Great and the Phony Clue**: Against ferocious cats, hostile adversaries, and a sly phony clue, Nate struggles to prove that he's still the greatest detective.

❑ **Nate the Great and the Sticky Case**: Nate is stuck with his stickiest case yet as he hunts for his friend Claude's valuable stegosaurus stamp.

❑ **Nate the Great and the Missing Key**: Nate isn't afraid to look anywhere—even under the nose of his friend's ferocious dog, Fang—to solve the case of the missing key.

- **Nate the Great and the Snowy Trail**: Nate has his work cut out for him when his friend Rosamond loses the birthday present she was going to give him. How can he find the present when Rosamond won't even tell him what it is?

- **Nate the Great and the Fishy Prize**: The trophy for the Smartest Pet Contest has disappeared! Will Sludge, Nate's clue-sniffing dog, help solve the case and prove he's worthy of the prize?

- **Nate the Great Stalks Stupidweed**: When his friend Oliver loses his special plant, Nate searches high and low. Who knew a little weed could be so tricky?

- **Nate the Great and the Boring Beach Bag**: It's no relaxing day at the beach for Nate and his trusty dog, Sludge, as they search through sand and surf for signs of a missing beach bag.

- **Nate the Great Goes Down in the Dumps**: Nate discovers that the only way to clean up this case is to visit the town dump. Detective work can sure get dirty!

- **Nate the Great and the Halloween Hunt**: It's Halloween, but Nate isn't trick-or-treating for candy. Can any of the witches, pirates, and robots he meets help him find a missing cat?

- **Nate the Great and the Musical Note**: Nate is used to looking for clues, not listening for them! When he gets caught in the middle of a musical riddle, can he hear his way out?

❑ **Nate the Great and the Stolen Base**: It's not easy to track down a stolen base, and Nate's hunt leads him to some strange places before he finds himself at bat once more.

❑ **Nate the Great and the Pillowcase**: When a pillowcase goes missing, Nate must venture into the dead of night to search for clues. Everyone sleeps easier knowing Nate the Great is on the case!

❑ **Nate the Great and the Mushy Valentine**: Nate hates mushy stuff. But when someone leaves a big heart taped to Sludge's doghouse, Nate must help his favorite pooch discover his secret admirer.

❑ **Nate the Great and the Tardy Tortoise**: Where did the mysterious green tortoise in Nate's yard come from? Nate needs all his patience to follow this slow . . . slow . . . clue.

❑ **Nate the Great and the Crunchy Christmas**: It's Christmas, and Fang, Annie's scary dog, is not feeling jolly. Can Nate find Fang's crunchy Christmas mail before Fang crunches on *him*?

❑ **Nate the Great Saves the King of Sweden**: Can Nate solve his *first-ever* international case without leaving his own neighborhood?

❑ **Nate the Great and Me: The Case of the Fleeing Fang**: A surprise Happy Detective Day party is great fun for Nate until his friend's dog disappears! Help Nate track down the missing pooch, and learn all the tricks of the trade in a special fun section for aspiring detectives.

❑ **Nate the Great and the Monster Mess**: Nate loves his mother's deliciously spooky Monster Cookies, but the recipe has vanished! This is one case Nate and his growling stomach can't afford to lose.

❑ **Nate the Great, San Francisco Detective**: Nate visits his cousin Olivia Sharp in the big city, but it's no vacation. Can he find a lost joke book in time to save the world?

❑ **Nate the Great and the Big Sniff**: Nate depends on his dog, Sludge, to help him solve all his cases. But Nate is on his own this time, because Sludge has disappeared! Can Nate solve the case and recover his canine buddy?

❑ **Nate the Great on the Owl Express**: Nate boards a train to guard Hoot, his cousin Olivia Sharp's pet owl. Then Hoot vanishes! Can Nate find out *whooo* took the feathered creature?